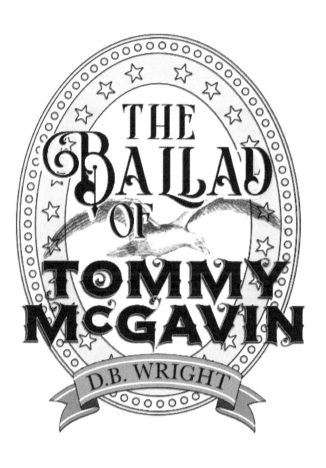

THE BALLAD OF TOMMY McGAVIN

D.B. WRIGHT

SCISSORTAIL PRESS

Stillwater, Oklahoma USA

ISBN: 978-1-955814-67-6

COVER & BOOK DESIGN BY BRIAN FUCHS

*This story is dedicated to my mother
and to my imagination, one of which is
responsible for the other.*

Image Credits

Acknowledgments

To all the writers, readers and dreamers of the world: you may feel like a dying breed, but I promise you are not.

Thanks to the people who helped keep this ship sailing: Shannon, Bibby, Mike, Emily, Brian

ONE

Two Ships, Two Ships
Both lost at sea.
Two Drinks, Two Drinks
We'll remember thee.

(Narrator)
At the Two Ships Tavern,
On the Old Shore Road,
Sat Tommy McGavin
A sight to behold.

Weathered and haggard,
Pasty and thin,
A sixty-year-old body
In ninety-year-old skin.

Hair like old dock ropes
Knotted and rust-red,
A beard like a mountain goat,
Framed a big turnip head.

He'd once been quite handsome,
So the fisher wives say,
Now his face paid the ransom
For too many wild days.

(Tommy)
"Gather 'round lads for I have a story
A most unearthly and peculiar tale!
Now you might think it jackanory
But I'm not talking through the Ale."

(Narrator)
The noise in the tavern
Whispered down from its yell
Whenever Tommy McGavin
Had anecdotes to tell.

Some rolled their eyes
And went back to their beers,
The rest they decided
To lend him their ears.

(Tommy)
"So, hear me out please,
And don't interfere,
Let me tell it complete,
Don't laugh and don't jeer.

It starts with me fishing
West of Old Carnlough Bay.
Weather glorious and baking
As usual most Mays.

Then happened this mystery
Most hard to explain.
In a flash it went misty
And down came hard rain.

I was taken aback,
Stunned and agog,
In no more than half minute
It went sunny to fog."

(Seamus)
"Impossible man!"
Offered Seamus with doubt
"Fog in half minute -
You've drank too much stout."

(Hearty)
"Come on now Seamus
Don't be a grouch
Tommy's barely beginning
Let's hear the man out."

(Tommy)
"In silence I waited
Confused in the mist,
Then out of the fog
Flew hundreds of fish.

I looked to me nets
And pulled on me ropes,
They jumped and hopped
Right into me boat."

(Seamus)
"Flying fishes ha-ha
Is your brain missing?
Never have I heard -"

(Hearty)
"-SHUSH let him finish."

(Tommy)
"I swear to all gods
this story is true.
Now hush up your gobs
And let me get through.

As I was just saying
The fishes jumped the boat;
So many kept coming
I was afraid it wouldn't float.

Coming flock after flock
With no sign of a cease.
I went to me tool-box
To fetch out me priest.

With that I started batting
As many I could see,
But the fish they kept arriving
In the boat and on me.

In no time at all
I was knee deep in fish,
Just a few fish more
And the boat it would tip."

(Seamus)
"This is ridiculous
He's having us on.
A boat full of fishes
Really? Come on."

(Tommy)
"You can take it or leave it
But there's truth to my tale.
If you're shocked by this first bit
The rest will turn you pale!"

(Seamus)
"I'm all ears Tommy, la,
But I have to tell truth,
Judging from so far
It seems like a ruse."

(Hearty)
"Maybe so matey
But I'm enjoying it no less.
Whether real or a fantasy
Let him tell us the rest."

TWO

Sure, Fish can fly
And pigs can too
But I wonder why
They're not in the zoo.

(Tommy)
"Much obliged me old brethren
Now if I could go on -
Where was me story at?
Oh, it's hardly begun!

Smothered so I was,
now up to me waist.
I tried with a heave
To escape fishy fate.

The old boat couldn't take it,
This new seafood weight.
She cracked and she creaked
Seemed destined to break.

I then sensed a churning;
A change of the sea.
T'was twisting and turning,
Growing wild and angry.

In all my years out there
I'd not seen it like this;
The sea oh so raging
And such a thick mist.

And the temperature lads
Went cold as fresh ice,
When a moment before
Was warm and nice.

The wind it picked up
From gusts to a gale.
Against my big mush
I could feel hard hail.

The waves were furious
A pack of angry wolves;
The air bit ferocious
Baying for blood.

Something came hurtling
From under me feet.
The boat it flew up
And crashed down with a fit."

(Seamus)
"Lifted? Come on now,
Sounds like a crock!
You just went off wayward,
You just hit on a rock."

(Tommy)
"Wait till you hear then
The rest I've to say;
I'm just at the start
So, hush now I pray.

For dear life I clung on
As the sea threw me 'round.
I was like a rag doll
Being tossed up and down.

My boat, poor old Bessy,
Could take no more pressure,
And right underneath me
The wood snapped a fissure.

One of the dock ropes
Whipped up with the force,
It caught 'round me throat
And was choking me horse.

At this point me laddies,
I'm not going to lie,
I thought that I'd had it,
'Twas my time to die.

Now, I'm not religious,
As I'm sure you all know,
But in that predicament
I gave prayer a go.

I prayed to the old gods
And mentioned some new.
I asked for salvation
And said my Adieu.

My life flashed before me
As the sea took me down.
It was all but for certain
I was fated to drown."

THREE

*Many a man
Has floundered at sea,
And many a man
Has fallen for thee.*

(Narrator)
Tommy leaned back
And let out a sigh,

(Tommy)
"Sure my eyes they are wet
And my mouth is so dry."

(Seamus)
"Ha! We should have guessed
His story's a front.
Whiskey and ale
Is all that he wants."

(Hearty)
"Be fair to the man
The story is hellish,
He's needing a drink
From having to tell it.

Here ya go me old pal
I'll shout you a tipple.
If the tale turns out well
I'll shout you a triple!"

(Tommy)
"Well, I wouldn't say no
To such a kind offer:
I can vouch you this story
It's truthful and proper."

(Narrator)
He swigged at the drink
Like a wounded old soldier.
His cheeks flushed to pink,
He stretched out his shoulders.

(Hearty)
"What happened next now?
Go on again please.
We're dying to know-
You've got us intrigued."

(Tommy)
"So, I was set for drowning
In this furious storm,
My death was approaching
All hope had withdrawn.

When a miracle happened
From below in the sea,
A bright white light
Was beaming at me."

(Seamus)
"Jaysus almighty
What drink did you pour?
It's sent him doo-lally
If he wasn't before!"

(Hearty)
"Can you stop interrupting
I'm desperate to hear.
The pub will be shutting
If we don't lend our ears."

(Tommy)
"This bright light lads
It was blinding and fierce,
And there was this noise
That pierced at me ears.

It rose all around me
The sound and the light,
Bleaching the seascape
And purging my fright.

I felt in that moment
Warm, safe and sound.
Somehow, I knew that
I wouldn't be drowned.

Now lads, I'll be honest
The story now twists.
It'll be hard to believe,
I have to admit."

(Seamus)
"I'll tell you now Tommy,
Since we're being so sincere,
From you opened your mouth
Your head's not seemed clear.

But I have to be fair
The story is delivering.
So please don't stop there
The action is gripping!"

(Tommy)
"My head went all woozy,
All slow in my brain.
I felt like pure morphine
Had entered my veins.

As I fought for my senses
I could hardly believe it,
From out of the sea rose
A beautiful mistress!"

(Seamus)
"It's confirmed boys
He has lost the plot.
Call Doctor Burns,
Ring for the cops!"

(Tommy)
"Ah lads I can see
You won't let me conclude.
I'm going to cease
If you'll keep being rude."

(Hearty)
"He's joking for sure,
Aren't you now Seamus?
Come carry on now
You're entertaining us"

(Tommy)
"I understand the doubts,
I promise I do.
If I were in your seat
I'd doubt it all too.

"So there I was useless
Limp, warm and woozy,
With a beautiful goddess
Hovering towards me."

"To describe her appearance
Would do her disservice,
Like an angel had fallen
To give me deliverance.

Light bounced around her
As if under her dominion.
She glinted and shined
And gleamed of perfection.

I thought that this angel
Had come for my soul,
To take me to heaven
To join Molly and Cole.

"She held up her hand
And pointed a finger,
Then screamed a command,

(Branwen)
'OUT THE WAY GINGER'"

FOUR

Oh Daughter, oh daughter
Of the great seas;
Oh daughter, oh daughter
Shine your light on me.

(Narrator)
Tommy took pause
And reached for his mug,
Through his untidy beard
He took a big glug.

(Tommy)
"There we was maties,
In the now calming sea,
Me and this maiden,
Who was screaming at me!

Then she snatched at my arm
Lifted me clean from the briny.
Her grip was white warm
And tingled right through me.

She held me like that,
The way a child holds a teddy,
Then cast me aside,
With almost no energy."

(Seamus)
"A flying fair maiden
With strength of ten guys
You've told some tall tales,
But this takes the pie."

(Tommy)
"I flew through the air,
spinning and flopping,
Thirty feet or much more
'Till I came down splashing.

As I flapped in the water
I still felt her heat.
I came to the surface
Not gasping to breathe!

I gathered my mind
And control of my limbs,
Then spied with my eyes
A second magic being."

(Seamus)
"Oh now there's two of the buggers
For the price of just one." -

(Hearty)
- "Hush for Christ sake
I'm listening to Tom!"

(Seamus)
"Listening to madness
Is what is more like," -

(Hearty)
-"well have you away then
Get on your bike."

We're Sorry there Tommy
For breaking your flow.
I'll shout you a whisky.
Please, on you go!"

(Tommy)
"There was two of them now
Stood atop the water.
One was the angel,
A huge man the other.

He was 15 foot high
And as wide as I'm tall,
Like one of those statues
To commemorate old wars.

His skin, hair and beard
Were all shades of grey-bronze.
His attire slimed and mudded
Like he'd slept in a pond.

His clothes hung all shredded
Tattered and torn
On top of his head
Was a busted-up crown.

I treaded the briny
As best my limbs could.
The man in me frightened,
The child in me awed.

The giants started talking
With loud booming voices.
The woman who'd saved me
Seemed utterly furious.

(Branwen)
'HOW NOW MANANNAN
WHAT IS THIS TREACHERY?
YOU'VE ALLOWED THIS HUMAN
TO BARE WITNESS TO ME!'

(Manannan)
'SISTER YOU INSULT ME
I'M HERE FOR HIS SOUL
AS IS MY PREROGATIVE
UNDER SAILOR GOD CODE.'

(Branwen)
'LAST TIME I HEARD
COLLECTION REQUIRES DEATH
HE'S LIVING AND BREATHING
DID YE NOT BOTHER TO CHECK?'

(Tommy)
"The man-god zoomed forward
Quick as a flash.
He grabbed me towards him
Stuck his nose in my face."

"He studied me intently
With a grimace and frown.
Then asked a strange question,

(Manannan)
'WHY DIDN'T YE DROWN?'

(Tommy)
"I couldn't utter a word.
Fear caught me tongue.
I squeaked out a gargle,
squeezed from me lungs."

(Manannan)
'THIS IS A RARE ONE
I HAVE TO CONFESS.
ARE YOU TOMMY MCGAVIN?'

(Tommy)
"S-s-s-ir, I am yes."

(Manannan)
'WELL, OH WELL TOMMY
THIS HERE'S A FINE MESS.
YOU'RE THE FIRST ONE IN CENTURIES
THAT MANAGED TO CHEAT DEATH!'

(Tommy)
"I-I-I don't know your meaning,
Really I d-d-don't.
I was just out here fishing,
Me and m-m-my boat."

(Manannan)
'DID YOU SPARE HIS LIFE SIS?
YOU'VE DONE IT BEFORE!'

(Branwen)
'DON'T BE RIDICULOUS
SPARE HIM - WHAT FOR?'

(Tommy)
"This is a mix up,
Some kind of mistake.
I'm sure I can fix it
Back at the bay."

(Manannan)
'IF IT WERE SO SIMPLE
IT WOULD ALREADY BE DONE.
I FEAR YOUR ADVENTURE
HAS ONLY JUST BEGUN.'

MY FINE, FAIR, FIERCE SISTER
THE OLD GODS DID DECIDE,
WHEN YOU BORE WITNESS TO HER,
THAT SHE'D BE YOUR GUIDE.'

(Branwen)
'THIS IS A TRAVESTY!
YOU'LL PAY FOR THIS MANNY!
THERE'S SOMETHING AT PLAY;
SOME UNDERHAND TRICKERY.'

(Manannan)
'HE WAS SET TO DECEASE
AND WAS SUDDENLY SPARED.
WHETHER ACCIDENT OR PURPOSE
WAS BY YOU HE WAS SAVED.'

(Branwen)
'&@£&?, @&£#$>$@&£
¥$€#@&?& @?£&*+$@€
£&! &#%+€@ $$% @&£
}#%¥$@& @& €$ #%¥'

(Manannan)
'SISTER SUCH LANGUAGE
IN FRONT OF THIS GENT.
WIND IN THAT TONGUE
IT'S NO TIME TO VENT.'

THE OLD GODS THEY SAY
ARE FULL OF WISE WITS,
HAVE MYSTERIOUS WAYS,
AND DEVIOUS TRICKS.

THERE'S NO TIME TO DITHER
YOU MUST GET HIM AWAY.
ARAWN WILL COME HITHER
WITH A PRICE TO BE PAID!'

FIVE

At the sharpness of each cold dusk
And tenderness of each new dawn.
From out of ashes and wandering dust
We pray our souls received, Arawn.

(Narrator)
The Two Ships Tavern
Had gotten quite rowdy,
Old Tommy McGavin
Had people talking loudly.

The landlord was worried
At the increase in tension.
What was expected
When Lord Death gets mentioned?

(Hearty)
"Tommy my good Patron
I'm loving this here story
But mentioning Arawn
Can be taken quite sorely.

Will you not tell the others
The story's just fiction?
If we don't calm them down
There's going to be friction."

(Tommy)
"What can I tell ya?
I speak as I remember.
I can stop in my yarn,
But my words I won't censor."

(Seamus)
"Well, let's keep more hushed
Between just ourselves.
You can whisper the rest
To those close around."

(Tommy)
"My throat's dry and grisly
Causing me to shout.
I could use a wet whistle
On some of the best stout"

(Hearty)
"Ha! it's a deal,
I'll set up the barrel.
I'll offer it to all
To calm down the rabble.

Come on ya bold thugs
Let's calm it right down.
I'm cracking some good stuff
And passing it round."

(Narrator)
The offer was met
With whistles and cheers.
That's what you get
When you hand out free beers.

With the ambience now calmed
By bribing the customers,
Tommy continued his yarn
But now it was whispered.

(Tommy)
"The goddess stared me down
With a look of disgust,
Then I registered a sound
Like a rock scratching rust.

It screeched through my brain
And jangled my nerves.
It was causing her pain
She started to squirm."

(Manannan)
'HE'S UPON US ALREADY,
YOU MUST BE LEAVING.
GO NOW WITH TOMMY,
I'LL STAY HERE TO STALL HIM.

(Branwen)
'I'VE DONE NOTHING WRONG
SO, WHY SHOULD I FLEE?
LET'S STAND OUR GROUND
WHAT'S THE WORST IT CAN BE?'

(Manannan)
'BRANWEN, STUBBORN SISTER
YOU KNOW AS WELL AS I DO,
IN LIEU OF AN ANSWER
IT'S BANISHMENT FOR YOU.

SEEK OUT THE ORACLE
FIND HOW TO ATONE.
THERE MUST BE AN ANSWER
WRITTEN IN THE STONES.'

(Tommy)
"She let out a growl
Stormy and frightening
Her face was like thunder
Her eyes were like lightning.

From those oceanic eyes
Sparked a crackle of light.
She started to rise
And then we took flight.

We whizzed over the sea
At a pace I can't guess,
Her clutching me
Like a babe to her breast.

The speed was so fierce
The air bit at my face.
Sounds howled in my ears
Like ghosts in the waves.

Amongst all the roar
I could still hear that buzz,
The one from before
Like rocks scratching rust.

It seemed to get closer
Despite our great pace.
Louder and louder
The noise gave us chase.

I could feel that the blare
was hurting poor Branwen.
Light crackled around her,
Her body was shaking.

And not just the noise
Was following our route.
It seemed a harsh darkness
Was giving us pursuit.

I scoped the horizon
And saw its approach.
A cloud of dark demons,
A flock of black ghosts.

Amongst the dour herd
I thought I could spy
A shape like a shepherd,
Looming up to the sky.

This odious pursuer
One conclusion I could draw-
It was he and no other:
The Underlord, Arawn."

SIX

A sacrifice given
Is gratefully received,
A sacrifice hidden
Is hardly perceived.

(Narrator)
At the Two Ships Tavern,
On the Old Shore Road,
Sat Tommy McGavin
Eyes owlish and old.

The Silence from his buddies
You could have cut with blades.
Lost in hearing the story
Their banter had faded.

Seamus broke the stillness
As only he was able:

(Seamus)
"Tommy, you're killing us
With this here wild fable!

What a mind you've got.
Such a vivid imagination.
These words you concoct
Should be in a publication."

(Tommy)
"I wish it was concoction,
that none of it was true,
But it's real recollection
I'm telling here to you."

(Hearty)
"Let's not fall out, mates
More drinks I'll be pouring.
Tommy, tell us more
Of your riveting story."

(Tommy)
"I say Amen to that
And cheers to you brothers
Now where was I at?

(Seamus)
"Awarn" Seamus whispered.

(Tommy)
"The noise kept increasing
In pitch and in pain,
The incessant screeching
Was grating me brain.

The darkness was closing,
It's mist taking forms,
Demonic black figures
With red eyes and horns.

Branwen was suffering
Her pace began to slow,
Her aura evaporating,
And her eyes were aglow.

Closer and closer, boys
The darkness drew near,
And within the white noise
Voices I could hear.

The language or dialect
I couldn't make out
But the insidious intent
Was without any doubt.

The demonic voices
Whinnied and wailed.
The odious figures
Continued to gain.

From out of the darkness
Shot strings of black mist,
Like long twisting fingers
Reaching out for us."

(Hearty)
"The tendrils of Arawn
We've all read of this.
One touch from them
And you're cursed to abyss!"

(Tommy)
"Tendrils, they were, yes
When I think of it now.
That describes them best,
Black tendrils from hell.

They twisted and writhed,
Through the air they slinked.
They left trailing behind
Streams of black inky mist.

The light around Branwen
Was torching out heat
I could feel her touch burning
From head to me feet.

The tendrils they slashed
And lashed through the air,
Searching for the gaps
A chance to rip and tear.

Branwen's white hot glow
Fended off most attacks,
But, every once a while,
I'd feel my skin snap.

It felt like being stung
By thousands of wasps,
Poisonous prodding prongs
Agonisingly hot.

I grimaced and squealed
With each needle blow,
But my trauma was healed
By Branwen's warm glow.

But with each fended attack
Branwen's pace was slowed,
Her energy being sapped
And fading her glow.

The darkness was upon us
Its minions at our heels.
I prayed for deliverance
From the hellish ordeal.

Branwen further faltered
Her energy expended.
'Twas now very obvious
The chase it was ending.

She came to a stop
And fell to her knees;
I almost was dropped
Down Into the sea.

She was breathing like a horse
After a long hard race,
Loud panting and wheezing
And wincing with pain.

Surrounded by blackness,
Me lay in her arms,
We waited to be taken,
Swallowed by the dark.

But she wasn't quite ready
To give up to the dark.
Second wind found her belly
And back came her spark.

In a great feat of exertion
She focused her might,
And burst out an explosion
Of dazzling hot light."

(Seamus)
"Christ alive McGavin
She blew you both up?
So, tell me this now man-
Why weren't ye cooked?"

(Hearty)
"Why'd you butt in,
Seamus you villain?
Spoiling his Rhythm
Just when 'twas thrilling."

(Seamus)
"Yeah, yeah I'm so sorry,
It's just such a tall tale.
It wouldn't surprise me
If up popped a giant whale.

Or maybe a unicorn
Appeared from the sea,
And you and dear Branwen
Ride off and marry!"

(Tommy)
"Mock me as you may,
Make jest and have crack
At the end of the day
The story is facts"

(Hearty)
"Seamus being Seamus.
He's pulling ya chain.
Go on now and tell us,
Continue the tale."

(Tommy)
"Well, after the explosion
All time seemed to freeze.
Nothing was moving
Even the darkness ceased.

Some wild incantation
Had stopped all the world,
And only me and Branwen
We're spared from the curse.

We could move around freely
While all else was paused
Her tired hands still held me
For how long wasn't sure.

She took a deep breath
And exhaled with a creak.
With a crunch in her chest
She started to speak."

(Branwen)
'LISTEN NOW MORTAL
HEED ME REAL CLOSE.
I HAVE MERE MOMENTS
OF FIGHT IN MY SOUL.

TO GET TO THE ORACLE
TAKE FROM ME THIS STONE.
TO END US THIS TROUBLE
YOU MUST GO IT ALONE.

ITS HEAT IS LIKE A COMPASS.
ITS LIGHT WILL BE YOUR GUIDE.
DON'T TRY HARD TO FOCUS,
LET THE MAGIC DECIDE.

TAKE ALSO THIS CHAIN,
WEAR IT AROUND YOUR NECK.
AS LONG AS HOPE REMAINS
FROM DARKNESS IT PROTECTS.'

(Tommy)
"Then she threw back her head,
Started to mutter and chant,
Ancient words I'd never heard
But I sensed what they meant.

Her skin crackled and glowed,
Her body started shaking.
From light in her hands
She weaved a bright basket.

She set it on the sea
And placed me within,
Then spoke down to me

(Branwen)
'DON'T LET US DOWN GINGE.'

(Tommy)
"She pushed me away
With other-worldly force.
I slid over waves
On a mystery course.

I spied a very tragic sight,
Looking back as I departed;
Branwen faded out her light
And stepped into the darkness."

SEVEN

*It's cold, it's cold
Poor Cole, poor Cole
I'll give him a hug
Protect his sweet soul.*

-

*It's cold, it's cold
Poor Cole, poor Cole
I'll give him my heart
Warm and old.*

(Narrator)
At the Two Ships Tavern
On the Old Shore Road,
Old Tommy McGavin
Bid his friends cheerio.

(Tommy)
"Would you look at the time, boys
I must get me going.
I'll continue this story
Back here in the morning."

(Seamus)
"Are you joking us Tommy, la -
You're heading off home?"

(Tommy)
"Sure, I'm off to graveyard
To see Molly and Cole"

(Seamus)
"Ah, I'm sorry Tommy
Sure, I didn't know
Sweet Cole, lovely Molly
God rest their souls"

(Narrator)
Unsteady with alcohol
Tommy wobbled to his feet,
Bid his final farewell
And headed out to the street.

He stumbled from the pub,
Ruffled his big coat,
And started his journey
Along the Old Shore Road.

His injured old knee
Ached as he walked.
Slow and unsteady
He headed off north.

Past the old church
Through Little Cranny Alley
Past Bumblebee Park
And on to the cemetery.

There Tommy stood
For the rest of that evening.
Amongst dirty stones
Their shrine was gleaming.

It had been Twenty years
Almost to the day
Since dear Molly and Cole
Were taken away.

'Unavoidable accident'
That's what they all say,
From villages all around
People mourned and prayed.

For quite a long while
There was nowt heard from McGavin.
He locked himself away
And fell in to a depression.

He blamed himself
For the terrible tragedy,
Beat himself up
Drank himself silly.

Then one summers day,
In the middle of August,
He emerged from dismay,
And began re-existence.

He still drank too much
But at least he was social.
He still blamed himself
But was back on the ocean.

He fished and he drank
He drank and he fished
Told stories and sang
With the boys at 'Two Ships'.

On days that were hard
He drank more than fishing.
For days at a time
He'd often go missing.

And that was his life
Old Tommy McGavin
His only delight
Was The Two Ships Tavern.

EIGHT

Seven herrings, a salmon's fill;
Seven salmon, a seal's fill;
Seven seals, a large whale's fill;
Seven whales, a cirein-cròin's fill.

(Narrator)
At the two ships tavern,
The very next morning,
A hungry McGavin
Turned up for a feeding.

He feasted on gammon
Sausage, eggs and beans,
And washed it all down
With a pint of cheap mead.

Then out from the cold
Freezing and flustered,
Seamus arrived,
Cheeks crimson blustered.

(Seamus)
"Morning there Tommy."
He greeted with a smile
"Good to see you up early
Did your visit fair well?"

(Tommy)
"It was what it was,"
Said Tommy with sorrow
"They were dead yesterday,
Still will be tomorrow."

(Narrator)
Seamus knew better
Than to press on the point,
Instead he decided
To offer Tommy a pint.

(Seamus)
"Drink my old muck-
To ward off this cold?"

(Tommy)
Tommy perked up
"Well I won't say no!"

(Seamus)
"Two drinks here Hearty
And breakfast for me
I'll be sitting in that seat
With me old mate Tommy"

(Narrator)
As Seamus joined Tommy
He patted his back
Smiled with sympathy
Then quietly they sat.

Hearty the landlord
Arrived with food and drinks
As he placed them down
He gave Tommy a wink.

(Hearty)
"So, Tommy your adventure,
I'm desperate to hear more.
Would you give us a chapter
Before you leave shore?"

(Tommy)
"Sure, don't see why not
I could use the distraction
Now where had I got -
Which place in the action?"

(Seamus)
"Arawn" whispered Seamus,
"Had just taken Branwen,
But she'd saved your ass
Before she was taken."

(Tommy)
"Ah yes, that's right!
My brave goddess Branwen
Had self-sacrificed
To rescue McGavin!

She created a basket
Forged from pure light,
And with me inside it
Pushed with such might.

I drifted away
For how long I can't say-
It could have been hours
Or might have been days.

Time became a blur,
My mind all fuzzy.
The sun stung and burnt,
Sea winds attacked me.

I was jolted and shook
As the basket hit landmass,
Shaken and shocked
Confused and harassed.

It took me a while
To find all me senses,
Some parts of me whined
Other bits were cursing.

I managed at last
To crawl from the basket.
So grateful I was that
It wasn't my casket.

I rubbed at my eyes
And looked all around,
A huge rock island
Was what I had found.

But the rock wasn't rough
Like you'd expect,
It was rubbery to touch.
It didn't feel correct.

As I rose to my feet
I felt a feint shake,
The rock underneath
Grumbled and quaked.

It was like a loud snore
Which quickly grew,
And suddenly boys
The rock it moved!"

(Seamus)
"Hah! A moving rock -
Will ya listen to him?
Last time I checked
Rocks they don't swim."

(Tommy)
"Well, I'm telling you now,
If you'd hush up and listen,
The rock I was stood on
It started just drifting.

My trusty old sea legs
Wobbled and shook.
The rock picked up speed
And I fell on me butt.

So, there I was boys
Ass about face,
This turbo charged boulder
Gathering pace.

As the speed got swifter
I was rolling and sliding.
I searched for something
To stop me from slipping.

Then I noticed a hole
Cut into the rock,
Something to hold
And stop me falling off.

I battled and scrapped
'gainst sea spray and spit,
And with all I had left
Hauled myself to the pit.

There in the hole
I found some relief.
Wind further howled
Velocity increased.

Just as I was thinking
I was safe and secure
The hole I was sat in
Bubbled and roared.

Then it opened up,
Like a great big mouth,
And with a sudden rush
A great geyser burst out"

(Seamus)
"Ha! I knew it see-
A big giant whale;
I told you there'd be
A whale in this tale.

(Hearty)
"Well aren't you a genius?
You are just the best!
Now can you be letting us
Listen to the rest?"

(Tommy)
"I'll continue now laddies
Despite ya harsh doubts;
You can make it up to me
With a pint of that stout.

I was thrown to the sky
On a furious fountain,
Who knows how high,
Seemed up with the mountains.

Then came the fall
As the fountain ceased,
From a height that tall
I'd sure be dead meat!

Inches from the surface
Of the great whale beast
The water re-surged
In time to catch me.

And back up I went
On a new gush of water,
And as I came down
I met the next geyser.

Thrown again,
Up to the sky,
Down again,
Caught just in time.

Down and up,
Up and down,
The beast laughing,
Me with a frown.

This went on maties,
For what felt like a day,
Until the cruel whale
Was done with its play.

It ended its cruel laughter
And let out a long sigh,
With a huge final geyser
Sent me up to the sky.

This time was so high,
Beyond even the clouds,
T'was a beautiful sight
'til I pondered coming down.

I started to plummet
From such a great height-
It seemed I was finished
Death was in sight.

The air it howled
Around skin and bones,
I closed my eyes
And prayed as I dove.

The ground got closer
My heart had stopped
It would be soon over
I'd land with a splosh!

And then my buddies
The next miracle occurred,
From out of the clouds
Appeared a huge bird."

(Seamus)
"Now it's the birds!
They're giant too?
What will be next
A giant baboon?"

(Narrator)
Tommy ignored
Seamus' jeer,
He rolled his eyes
And glugged his beer.

(Tommy)
"Thirty foot wide
At least was this gull;
It's beak was the size
Of a fishing boat hull.

And stranger than that,
What amazed me the most:
The bird was see-through
Like an avian ghost!

Towards me it swooped
And clutched me in talons,
Then let out a squawk:

(Giant Bird)
'I WAS SENT BY MANANNAN.'"

(Hearty)
"Mannanan's gull
I've heard of this myth,
The spirit of a bird
Given as a gift."

(Seamus)
"A giant talking bird
That's also a ghost
Did you use special herbs
On old Tommy's toast?"

(Tommy)
"The bird glided downwards
With me held in its claws,
Towards nearest landfall
Heavens knows where that was.

It dropped me with a thud
On to pearly white shore,
Then it flew away up
Letting out a warm caw."

NINE

Vates, the void watcher:
Observing past and future,
The knower and the seer,
Universal truth seeker.

(Tommy)
"This shore I was at
I didn't know it at all,
None of the maps
Would show it, I'm sure."

(Seamus)
"A shore off the maps,
D'ya mean in ya head?
Seems convenient that
And full of pretence!"

(Tommy)
"I looked all around me
And nothing made sense.
The blueness of the sea.
Hot air was so dense.

Such a heat there was lads
Sweat dripped from my skin.
The bushes and plants
We're foreign and thin.

T'was like I'd been transported
To a tropical climate;
An African shoreline
Or Caribbean Island.

(Seamus)
"Jaysus McGavin
How far had you travelled?
I think all that sunshine
Has your brain scrambled."

(Tommy)
"I can tell you as it was
That's all I can do,
You can sneer and judge
But this is the truth.

T'was perfectly clear
I needed out of the sun,
In a matter of hours
I'd be cooked, over-done.

I could see shady trees
Over in the yonder,
Under them at least
I could find some shelter.

So, I headed in land
Away from the beach,
Grass replaced sand
Underneath me feet.

I was approaching the trees,
When a noise caught me ears,
The one from the seas
It filled me with fears.

Like rusty old chains
Scraping against rocks,
Or the screeching bird screams
When you startle a flock.

And there in the distant,
Amidst the heat haze,
I spied someone watching
A figure cloaked in grey.

Beside the dark figure
There were two great beasts
With albino white fur,
Grinning huge bloody teeth.

Their eyes glowing rubies,
Their ears blood red,
Against pale white bodies,
And sharp pointed heads"

(Hearty)
"Awarn's undead hounds,
We all know this legend;
They chase your soul down
And tear it asunder."

(Tommy)
I felt tingles of pain
From the chain on my neck:
'AS LONG AS HOPE REMAINS
FROM DARKNESS IT WILL PROTECT'.

Arawn, he was watching
But he couldn't approach,
As long I was wearing
The guardian broach.

The stone in my pocket -
The one from dear Branwen -
It started vibrating,
Scorching and burning.

I reached in me trousers
And fished the stone out
It was too hot to handle
So, I threw it to the ground.

It glowed so bright,
Like the glare of the sun,
Then it hopped head high
And it buzzed and hummed.

Light trailed behind it
As it hopped along weeds,
Quite slowly at first,
Then took off at speed.

I recalled Branwen's words
'ITS LIGHT WILL BE YOUR GUIDE'
And knew I should follow
So, I ran alongside.

We raced through the trees
Deeper into woods,
Aches in me knees
Hot burn in me lungs.

That's when I noticed
We were being stalked,
Skittering creatures
Shuffling towards us.

All kinds of vermin
We're in our pursuit,
I could hear the pattering
Of thousands of feet.

The stone led a path
To the bank of a river,
We ran along the bank
As creatures drew nearer.

The chitter and chatter
Of teeth and claws,
Starving arachnids
Desperate to gorge.

The river arrived
At a great waterfall,
The creatures behind
Almost had us caught.

The stone disappeared
Behind the falling water;
It left me for dead,
McLamb to the slaughter.

Pincers and fangs
Flickered and snapped-
I said a quick prayer
And hoped I'd die fast.

From out of nowhere..
Came a bang and a flash,
Blue smoke filled the air
And the beasts scattered back.

The Smoke faded away
Revealing an old woman,
Crinkled skin, hair pale-grey,
Like a witch from a coven.

The stone was bouncing
Around at her feet:
This was The Oracle
The person I seeked-"

"Are you-" (Tommy)

(Vates)
'Yes, I am her,
Her is me,
She be her,
Me be she.

Vates I am,
Vates the great.
Great I am,
The GREAT VATES.

Blah blah blah,
So on, so forth.
Yadda yadda,
What you here for?'

(Tommy)
"Um. Tommy I am
Tommy McGavin,
I'm a fisherman,
Sent on a mission."

(Vates)
'McGravel, Mcfartface,
Whatever, who cares?
You turn up at my place
Unannounced, unawares.

Listen McDaftone
I'll ask more CLEAR,
Answer this question:
WHY are you HERE?'

"The stone it-" (Tommy)

(Vates)
'Oh yes, Stones! ALWAYS stones,
Leading people to my lair.
No doubt t'was an Under-God
Who bid that you come here?'

"Well, yes-" (Tommy)

(Vates)
"GO AND SEEK THE ORACLE'
They're always saying that,
Like I've nothing better to do
Than deal with inane crap.'

"I'm sorry I just-" (Tommy)

(Vates)
'Don't say you're sorry
It means less than naught.
Tell me McGobbo
How did this all start?'

"I was ju- (Tommy)

(Vates)
'Just on your boat
Minding your business,
They all say that
All of them innocent.

And old muggins here
Has to clean up the mess.
I've a good mind my dear
To turn you to mush.'

"Please-" (Tommy)

(Vates)
'Well, you'd better come
And follow old Vates,
See what can be done
About your harsh fate.'

(Tommy)
"I followed this witch
Deep in to the caves,
Only flame on a stick
Lighting the way.

There were dreadful noises
From beasts out of sight,
I dare not imagine
What they looked like.

Eventually we arrived
Upon a shimmering room,
Crystals and candles
Flickered through gloom.

The room was filled up
With pink-violet smoke,
Shelves of battered books,
Jars fractured and broke.

In the middle of the floor
Was a huge black cauldron,
Simmering up odours
Like flower scented sulphur."

(Vates)
'Welcome, welcome
To my humble hovel,
Sit yourself down
And cause no bother."

I'll fetch us some tea,
It's green and tastes bad.
You can take it or leave it
What better offer you had?

I can give you food
But doubt you'd be partial;
I eat rats and shrooms
Bats if I can catch 'em.'

(Tommy)
"It sounds delicious
But I don't think I will.
To tell you the truth
I'm feeling a touch Ill."

(Vates)
'Suit yourself McGravy
No difference to me
Visitors this century
Are so bloody fussy.'

(Tommy)
"She sidled to a pantry
And was back in a flash,
With a big pot of tea
And a basket of rats.

She plucked a rat
From out of the basket
Tilted her head back
And started to eat it."

(Seamus)
"Urgh! Sure now Tommy
Did you have to tell that bit?
I've not long had breaky
You've made me feel sick."

(Tommy)
"Well, it was a real trauma
Seeing her gobble those rats,
But it's not that much worse
Than a Two Ships breakfast."

(Hearty)
"You cheeky old beggar
My breakfast is famous,
People come from far
To sample my flavours."

(Seamus)
"Sure, they've no other choice-
There's no other places.
You're famous alright
But not for ya flavours."

(Tommy)
"We're yanking your chain
Your food is delicious,
The minor stomach pains
Are worth the nutrition."

(Hearty)
"You pair of bad arses
I should bar you right now.
Get on with ya story
You ungrateful lout!"

(Tommy)
"We sat there a while
With the rats and the tea,
Then she winked and smiled
Through sharp bloodied teeth."

(Vates)
'Now then McFussypants
Let's turn to the cauldron.
A bit of MAAAAAGIC sand
Will show me the visions.'

(Tommy)
"She threw some sand
In to the cauldron,
And with her hands
Made demonic contortions.

Bursts of violet smoke
Rose from the pot,
And amongst the mist
Images popped."

(Vates)
'Ah! I see now McBigBonce
As clear as moony nights,
Ya didn't die just once
Ya passed away thrice.'

(Tommy)
"Thrice! Three times-
What do you mean?
I'm just this one Tommy,
So how can that be?"

(Vates)
'Yes, once ya did die,
That much is the truth,
But in three different ways
Staked, drowned and noosed.

The wood from the boat
Stabbed through ya chest,
An' ya drowned in the ocean
While rope choked ya neck.'

(Tommy)
"That doesn't seem right
Are you certain and sure?
From my toes to my eyes
I don't feel dead at all."

(Vates)
'Now listen up McGobshite
Don't you dare doubt me:
Three times ya did die,
Now ya soul's split in three.

I am the great Vates
I don't make any errors,
Well, there was some debate
That time I melted a fella.

But that's not important.
What matters is right now.
Right now I am adamant
Three deaths I did count.'

"What -" (Tommy)

(Vates)
'Questions, answers,
I'm sure there are many!
Truth is McCracker
It's unprecedented.'

"It's never - " (Tommy)

(Vates)
'Happened before?
Most certainly yes.
To someone so boring?
Probably never yet.

To find a solution
To such turn of events,
I can only imagine
You'll face a great test.'

"What kind-" (Tommy)

(Vates)
'What kind of a test
I hear you now ask:
This kind was mans first
And probably the last.'

"I don-" (Tommy)

(Vates)
'You don't understand,
Why aren't I surprised?
It's a test forged in sand,
An old-fashioned kind.'

"Wher-" (Tommy)

(Vates)
'Where must you go?
I'm glad that you asked:
Down at the shore
Where judgements are cast.'

"But-" (Tommy)

(Vates)
'Question me no more
I'm done with this ruse,
Look into my cauldron
To reveal the whole truth.'

(Tommy)
"She tossed some dust
In to her black cauldron,
Pink smoke rose up
And the room started spinning."

(Vates)
'What you will see
Are things yet to pass;
Who you must be
Is the question to ask.'

(Tommy)
"The smoke began
To infiltrate me mind,
Visions and sounds
Entered ears and eyes.

Such vivid scenes
Felt real as rain.
A waking dream
Played out in me brain."

TEN

Where matter has no end
And time no beginning,
The Fate God Morrigan
Rolls the die of decisions.
-
The test of all men,
The last and the first-
The great redemption;
The soul is purged.

(Ethereal Female Narrator)
The sea soaks us in glory,
Tempestuous and old.
Tell to it your story,
Vindicate your soul.

Lie your crimes at the shore line,
Wash away sinful desires.
Deeply breath heavenly air,
Transgressions are retired.

If the light it blinds you
Let that be your sign.
Luminance will find you
And guide you to a shrine.

There, two sirens wait for you,
Where sun meets sea meets sand,
Urging you to hear their tongue,
And take you by the hand.

One of these beings is gracious
And crafted of suns gold rays.
The other is a malevolent beast
With wicked shadowy ways.

To know one from the other
Requires the purest heart.
The sinful doomed to failure,
The virtuous have a start.

Fear not that you are neophyte
To such paranormal arts.
For judgment lies not in your mind
It's settled in your heart.

Which one of the maidens
Will this day you meet -
Will it be the hellion
A brutal banshee beast?

Or has the tide been kind today
And met you safe relief -
The one of graceful precious ways
Who takes you in safe sheaf?

Now you must approach the tide
And walk with unknown steps.
Upon you has arrived the trial
A simple, ancient test.

In front and behind you
Light and dark fade away.
Replaced by swirly grey hues
Of neither night nor day.

Distant clouds and far fields
Begin to fade and blemish,
Leaving only blurred remains,
And fuzzy outlined premise.

The world which you were born to
Is failing to persist,
And in this new and untold light,
Begins to un-exist.

In the beginning, or ending
Sometimes exists a place.
Exists perhaps not the wording
More like an intangible trace.

It lies between all known things,
And nothing all at once.
Where every thought or meaning
Rendezvous to dance.

Between life and death,
Lightness and dark,
Stillness of breath,
And the spark of new stars.

Within this ethereal realm
You find yourself unawake,
Pondering if it's paradise
Or heaven has forsake.

Soon, or later, there's nothing left
In sight or in mind's eye,
Except you, the light and shadow
Trapped in a bubbled shrine.

For seconds and forever
You spin in total stillness.
There seems to be a battleground;
Light versus the darkness.

The new world is blown away
As un-suddenly as tides make sand.
The old world returns to play
With warm and gentle plans.

Sitting on the hot wet sands,
Counting out white pebbles,
She clasps a few within her hand
And casts them out as fossils.

She points you to the yonder
And urges you with haste;
A wild white-horsed tsunami
Begins to bubble and race.

On heavy thighs and lungs
You start a frantic sprint,
And just as you are falling dead
You feel a sudden lift.

"Away and away, have you away"
Her voice urges your spirit.
"The mistress has been kind today"
"Come never back to visit"

She throws to you a parting prize
A stone as white as snow.
It radiates and stings your eyes
With bright crackling glows.

What brilliant mind or artists eye
Could replicate such perfection?
Rocks tossed at the coming tide
That ripple out her reflection.

ELEVEN

*The stones hold the memory
Of the first-born stars;
Their power is legendary
Their fate is a farce.*

(Narrator)
At the two ships tavern
On The Old Shore Road
Old Tommy McGavin
Sighed and groaned.

(Seamus)
"So was that it McGavin
The end of the story?
Your soul was saved
Oh, Joy and glory!"

(Tommy)
"Not quite boys;
There's more to be telling,
A twist and a turn
To a marvellous ending."

(Hearty)
"We cannot wait Tom:
Give us the rest!
Here's a free rum
To spark interest."

(Tommy)
"Thank you so much
Could you make it a double?
It'll stir memory up,
If it's not too much trouble."

(Hearty)
"Sure, as you like, Tom,
Coming up shortly;
There's plenty more rum
In exchange for story"

(Tommy)
"So, I found myself back
In the cave of Great Vates;
I was laid out flat
Covered in a cape.

I thought to myself
Had I dreamt the whole thing?
But I had in me hand
The stone from the beach."

(Vates)
'Ah, McSnoresloud
I see you have roused,
You didn't horribly drown,
Or get buried in the ground.

Many have visited
To take the great exam,
Most end up drifting
As decaying flotsam.'

(Tommy)
"I rubbed at my head
And blinked weary eyes,
Before I could speak
Vates read my old mind."

(Vates)
'Yes, yes, more questions
Let's get it over with-
The stone you posses
Is a stone of the witches.'

(Vates)
'Hag stones some call 'em
On account of the occult
Or holey stones some
Because of the hole.

Blah, blah, blah
Either noun is same,
After all McFarter
What's in a name?

This stone gifted to you
Is a scarce thing indeed
Rare as rocking-horse poo
A handful ever seen.'

"Okay-" (Tommy)

(Vates)
'Don't interrupt McStinky
While I'm having a babble.
Interrupting a witch
Can land you in trouble.

THAT stone McSpawny
Is Morrigan's Soul Stone-
It grants it's owner
Redemption of a soul.

Only one can exist
In any space-time -
You are the luckiest
McPerson alive!'

"So what do-" (Tommy)
(Vates)
'Did I not make it clear?
Don't break my flow.
The soul stone it gives
Back a lost soul.

Before you ask Vates
I'll clarify it for you,
It's a common mistake
To confuse the two.

It's a SOUL stone -
Clue is in the name.
A life and soul stone
They are not the same."

It'll save ya soul
Not save ya from death,
Redeem your essence
But not ya flesh.

There's beings McBasic
That aren't mortal like us
But the soul they are made of
Comes from same cosmic dust."

So, the stone may be used
On all beings with souls,
God, man or beasts,
Whatever fate folds.

The gods of the fates
Are an eccentric strange breed;
You can hardly predict
What intention they decree.

All I can tell ya
Is there's no set path,
When space-time beckons
The stone it will act.

Take the soul stone
And keep it safe,
At the right moment
Give in to its fate.

McGavin, since I like you,
I'll give you this advice,
The end result of fates
Is rarely very nice.

If I'm being totally honest
You've come further than most,
One in many millions
End up with a stone.

Well now McCrackpot
Let's get you home.
I can give you two options:
Teleport or boat."

Teleportation is quicker
But it could melt ya brain,
The boat is an adventure
And takes two hundred days.'

(Seamus)
"Teleportation?
That sounds handy.
This is it Tom
The peak of your fantasy."

(Hearty)
"Ah, come on now, Seamus,
Don't be such a lout.
Which did you choose Thomas:
Teleport or boat?"

(Tommy)
"Well, the boat was a story
For another time, boys.
For the sake of brevity
It was teleport I chose."

(Vates)
'Very well McMincemeat
Teleportation it is,
I should warn you right now
The experience is grim.'

(Tommy)
"She fetched from a cupboard
A bottle of green liquid;
It bubbled and burbled
As she unscrewed the lid."

(Vates)
'I just need to recall
The ancient scriptures-
If I get the words wrong
The spell will kill ya!"

Gyth makki Mala bukki
G'tharkus yinjan-zwarts:
I'm joking McGullible
There're no ancient words.

Step into this circle,
And try not to move,
The slightest of motion
Can leave ya brain boiled.

Joking, joking;
I'm yanking ya chain.
You might feel discomfort
But it won't boil ya brain.'

(Tommy)
"She poured the liquid
All around at my feet,
She blew on some dust -
The ground simmered and steamed."

The floor became fluid
And I started to sink,
My legs disappearing
Soon up to my chin!"

(Vates)
'Well, Goodbye McSunshine
It was fun while it lasted.
You've been given redemption
Will ya try not to waste it?'

(Tommy)
"I sank further into liquid.
My mouth, nose, and eyes,
Until the whole of me submerged
Into the green slime."

The slime was cold as ice,
Thick, dark and gloopy,
With sparks of dancing light,
Like emerald jelly.

I battled to swim
Seeking the surface,
When the lights went dim
And I fell unconscious.

The next thing I know
I wake up by the docks.
I was dry as a bone
Not even wet socks.

My brain was frazzled
Dizzy and nauseous,
As soon as I stood up
I instantly vomited."

(Seamus)
"Ha, there we are lads
He woke from a stupor-
None of it happened
He's just a wild drinker."

(Hearty)
"Now stop it Seamus
Be fair to Tommy
He's been so gracious
Telling us this story."

(Tommy)
"After such an ordeal
My head was a haze
I thought of Molly and Cole
So, I went to their grave"

(Seamus)
"God rest their souls
Cole and sweet Molly;
She'd a heart of gold
And Cole was so canny."

(Hearty)
"I toast a rum tipple
To Molly and Cole,
A small dedication
To their beautiful souls."

You have our condolences
Our good pal Tommy.
To Molly and Cole."

"To Cole and Molly." (Seamus/Hearty)

(Tommy)
"Thank you my laddies,
Your words warm my soul.
I miss them so badly-
Heaven holds them for now."

(Narrator)
Tommy took some time
To reflect on his losses,
Wiped a tear from his eye
And went back to the story.

(Tommy)
"After such a journey
The place I had to be
Was with Cole and Molly
Down at the cemetery.

I stood a long while
Wallowing in self-pity
Wondering why
God hadn't taken ME.

Then lads, the stone
It shook in my pocket;
The stone with the hole
It was making a racket.

A sudden thick mist
Came over the cemetery.
The temperature dipped
From warm to frigid.

A voice then whispered
From out the dark fog
It sounded like Branwen
But a mouth full of frog."

(Dark Branwen)
'HOW NOW GINGER
DID YOU THINK THIS WAS DONE?
I'VE COME TO DELIVER
YOU WHERE YOU BELONG.'

(Tommy)
"From out of the murk
Emerged a shadow woman,
Adorned with black smoke-
A dark version of Branwen.

Where light once thrived
Shadows now flocked.
The oceanic eyes
Were empty sockets.

Tendrils of black mist
Twisted from her skin
And shadows hissed
Where daylight met them.

I reached for the medallion
The one meant to protect,
I aimed it at dark Branwen,
But she didn't react."

(Dark Branwen)
'NICE TRY MORTAL FOOL
BUT I'M TOTALLY IMMUNE,
PERHAPS YOU RECALL
I GIFTED IT TO YOU?'

(Tommy)
"Branwen lurched forwards
And clutched my throat,
Lifted me skywards-
I started to choke.

The holey stone
Screamed to be heard
It shook and moaned
Blazed and burned.

So hot it became
It scorched through me trousers
And fell on the ground
Spitting out hot embers.

Branwen's eyes shifted
And she let out a gasp,
She released her grip,
I fell hard on the grass"

(Dark Branwen)
'A WITCHES STONE
UNUSED AND FRESH.
YOU REDEEMED A SOUL?
YOU FACED THE TEST?'

(Tommy)
"She took a leap forwards
And reached for the stone,
But invisible forces
Meant back she was thrown.

She let out a screech
Wild and angry,
Jumped back to her feet
And charged towards me.

I covered my face,
Tucked knees to my chest,
Desperately prayed
And hoped for the best.

Suddenly she halted
And fell to her knees
Blackness retreated
Replaced by light beams.

The Light and dark
Battled around her;
Shadows and sparks
Competed for power.

For a brief moment
The light took a lead
And out from the conflict
Branwen did speak."

(Light Branwen)
'TOMMY MCGAVIN
I BESEECH YOU PLEASE LISTEN
IT'S ME BRANWEN
I HAVE ONLY A FEW SECONDS

THE STONE ISN'T LIMITED
TO ANY SINGLE BEING
'TIS POSSIBLE TO TRADE IT
TO MAN, GOD OR BEAST.

PICK UP THE STONE
PLUNGE IT INSIDE ME
IT WILL FREE MY SOUL
FROM ARAWN'S CLUTCHES.'

(Tommy)
"As darkness clawed back
And took over Branwen,
I knew what to do, lads-
I was clear of my mission."

TWELVE

*The dread of mortal beings
Is not that they should die-
The real fear that slowly stings
Is that they never tried.*

(Narrator)
At the Two Ships Tavern,
On the Old Shore Road,
Sat Tommy McGavin
A sight to behold.

Weathered and haggard,
Pasty and thin,
A sixty-year-old body
In ninety-year-old skin.

He took a deep breath,
Rubbed his tired face,
Swigged from his glass
And silently prayed.

(Tommy)
"Well now me laddies
What a pleasure it's been.
Thanks for having me,
I must take my leave."

(Seamus)
"What, Is that it Tommy-
The end of your tellin'?
What about the cemetery,
The stone and Branwen?"

(Tommy)
"Well now you nuisance
I guess you'll never know.
This is comeuppance
For mocking me so."

(Hearty)
"Aw, come on Tommy,
Don't be so bitter,
Finish the story
We're desperate to hear."

(Tommy)
"There's no more to add,
That's all you'll be getting.
You called it a sham
So, what odds an ending?"

(Narrator)
Tommy stood up,
With an unsteady sway,
Walked out the pub,
Gave his mates a last wave.

The infancy of morning
Had given way to afternoon.
The cold air was clawing
But the sun was in bloom.

He headed off north
The same route as always,
The road along the shore
Then cut through alleyways.

The sea lapped at rocks
Driven by harsh winds.
Gulls spun in crazed flocks,
Strange events beginning.

Past the old church,
Through little cranny alley,
Past bumblebee park,
And on to the cemetery.

Back at the Tavern
Seamus was seething
Tommy had left them
Guessing the ending.

(Seamus)
"Curse Tommy McGavin
For his unfinished story,
I'll get my vengeance-
He'll regret his trickery."

(Narrator)
The doors burst open
Inviting cold breeze,
In rolled young Shep
Struggling to breathe.

(Shep)
"Oh, woe now my brethren
You'll never guess what!
They've found Tommy McGavin
Dead down by the docks."

(Seamus)
"Sure, you must be mistaken,
We were with him just now.
That there's another person
Of that I would vouch."

(Shep)
"Just now, At the Two Ships?
I'm afraid there's no way,
Doctor burns confirmed it,
He's been dead least three days."

(Narrator)
Hearty look puzzled,
Seamus was bemused,
As they heard from Shep
The incredible news.

(Seamus)
"But how is this possible?"
Seamus began.
"Was that some imposter
Who spun us that yarn?"

(Hearty)
"If that was an imposter
They deserve a prize-
That there was Thomas
Well and Alive."

(Seamus)
"Shep there's an error,
Tommy isn't dead.
Go tell the doctor
To check it again."

(Narrator)
Tommy knelt at the grave
Quietly sobbing,
Singing prayers of praise
For Cole and Molly.

Evening was stealing
It's way into day,
Tommy got moving
On his sad way.

With solemn footsteps
He left the cemetery
And headed west
Beyond the estuary.

The air was still.
The world was quiet,
Only lapping waves filled
The eeriest silence.

(Seamus)
"Burns, my good friend,
With the utmost respect,
Tommy was well alive,
Chatting at his best."

(Dr. Burns)
"I'm telling ya man
Just one more time,
That there was McGavin
Swept up by the brine.

And dead he was boys,
No doubt of that,
For at least a few days
I'm certain as Jack."

(Hearty)
"That being the case,
Then how was he here -
Spinning us a tale
And drinking my beer?"

(Dr. Burns)
"I can give you no answer
Nor would I dare try,
All I can tell ya
Is Tommy has died."

(Seamus)
"A mystery indeed Doc
Of that there's no doubt,
To tell you the truth
It's freaking me out"

(Narrator)
Tommy reaches the shore.
As the tide is turning,
The sea is furious
Crashing and churning.

As Tommy walks the beach
He feels age leave his body,
His ailments and injuries
Dissolve as old worry.

Amongst the far waves,
Out in the distance,
A giant geyser
Blasts up skywards.

Tommy feels better
Than he's ever before,
Like all of life's woes
Have lifted abroad.

Overhead in the sky
A huge bird flaps it's wings,
Riding on its mantle
Is Manannan The King.

They swoop past Tommy,
Greet him with a wave,
Then depart quickly
Out over the vales.

At the mid-point of the beach,
Stood on golden sands,
Four figures wait to greet
Where the Witch Rock stands,

One is Light Branwen
Returned to bright glory.
Standing beside her
Are Cole and Molly.

Figure number four
Waiting on the sand,
The Underlord Arawn
Lord of the Damned.

Arawn nods his head,
A measure of esteem.
Branwen curtseys,
Molly and Cole beam.

At the Two Ships Tavern
The patrons were mourning;
Old Tommy McGavin
Had told his last story.

(Seamus)
"Here's to Old Tommy
Our friend and companion,
May he join Cole and Molly
Up there in heaven."

(Narrator)
The patrons cheered
And raised their drinks
There were many tears
As the glasses clinked.

Tommy, Molly and Cole
Walk into the distance
The air around them glows
And their auras glisten.

(Arawn)
'SOMETIMES BRANWEN
THE MORTALS SURPRISE US
TOMMY MCGAVIN
WILL FIND LEGEND STATUS'

END

EPILOGUE

Three Ships, Three Ships
All lost at sea
Three Drinks, Three Drinks
We'll remember thee.

(Narrator)
At The Two Ships Tavern
On the old shore road
Hangs a photo of Tommy
Framed in white gold.

Every anniversary
A stranger comes to visit
To pay respects to Tommy
For redeeming her spirit.

She gives coins to the landlord
And bids the patrons be Merry,
With cheer and applause
To celebrate old Tommy.

The crowd at the tavern
Raise drinks to his memory
And honour McGavin
With a special Sea Shanty

(Multiple patron voices)
Tommy was a fishing man
A fishing man
A fishing man
Tommy was a fishing man
All day, all day.

Tommy was a Two Ships man
A Two Ships man
A Two Ships man
Tommy was a Two Ships man
Oh yay, oh yay.

Tommy was a family man
A family man
A family man
Tommy was a family man
Hoo-ray, hoo-ray

Tommy passed the test of man
The test of man
The test of man
Tommy passed the test of man
Oh yay, oh yay.

Tommy saved dear Branwen
He saved Branwen
He saved Branwen
Tommy saved dear Branwen
Hip hip, hoo-ray

THE WITCH CHRONICLES

– PART ONE –

OF BROKEN LIGHT

Of Broken Light

In a winter lost to cruel dismay,
a story cast in crueller fates.
  An un-pure maiden, curious and calm,
  very aware of her future harm.

She sets upon a journey new,
the task at hand known by few.
  A simple sack of simple foods,
  a little flask of a certain brew.

She is a hunter of the night,
she is a witch of broken lights.
  She seeks an evil forged in hell,
  it is her mission to expel.

A hellion harridan haunts the land,
seeding corrupted evil plans.
  The forests sting in noxious moss,
  birds only sing of pain and loss.

Zealous fools have ventured forth,
to claim the head and prove their worth.
  Each one has met a gruesome fate,
  much worse than any nightmares make.

So destiny calls to her again,
to cast the foulness far away.
  Not the first and not the last,
  no bag of gold rewards the task.

For she is cursed and duty bonded,
to fend the lands of evil absconded.
>   And that is so, and so she must,
>   towards next target cut and thrust.

She mounts her loved and trusted horse,
and heads towards the headlands north.
>   The journey is a treacherous kind,
>   but fear to her is naught but in mind.

The days they pass without event,
she rides and eats and rides again.
>   As she approaches the destination,
>   she orders home her trusty stallion.

She came upon the haunted hill,
draped in mist and whispered chills.
>   And, as the depth of darkness closed,
>   a primal fear inside her rose.

And in the darkest depths of night,
she thought to run but stayed to fight:
>   And as the siren song grew loud,
>   compliant knees touched the ground.

A ground so cold it freezes nerves,
a ground so hot the bones it burns.
>   Petrified muscles unable to move,
>   it seems she's bitten more than she can chew.

The heathen hag was malignant and strong,
a demon fed from powerful throngs.
>   She hadn't expected this fierce foul foe,
>   the wretched enemy had seethed and grown.

She finds the will to give muscles motion,
and from her pocket grabs the potion.
    With chug and glug she consumes,
    and thus metamorphosis ensues.

Wild screams and savage roars,
pierce the air as she transforms.
    The hell spawn reels in shock and awe,
    then licks its lips and extends its claws.

"At last they sent a worthy one,
A witch no less this should be fun."
    The vicious demon starts an assault,
    lashing out towards the throat.

Our heroine is quick to react,
her new-found form is agile and fast.
    A dodge aside, and a counter slash,
    send the beast reeling back.

The hellion howls then fills its lungs,
in crimson rage comes another lunge.
    The beast is swift, our heroine quicker,
    nether-the-less a claw does catch her.

She winces and whines through gritted breath,
the claw had dug in to her flesh.
    Pain shot from the gruesome wound,
    a reminder that she wasn't immune.

The demonic hag let out a cackle,
 and gloated with a mocking babble:
    "One strike each, how much fun is this?
    Before sunrise your meat I'll feast"

"I applaud the drawing of my blood,
a feat no other creature could.
        But now the playtime it must end,
        back down to hell you'll send"

And then a final fight takes place,
a fierce, frenzied frantic haze.
        A mix of magic and raw brute force, a
        melee of smoke, teeth and claws.

Over many hours, or maybe days,
the thrash of battle wildly rages.
        Until at last the bedlam fades,
        the heat of conflict dissolved away.

In the aftermath remains one breath,
the heaving in our heroine's chest.
        Battle scarred, bruised and bleeding;
        she stands astride the fallen demon.

In a demonstration of found respect,
she bows before it and strokes its neck.
        And then with a final show of ferocity,
        she rips off the head to claim her trophy.

And all that remains of the mission,
is to purge the land of nocuous emissions.
        The forest birds she can already hear,
        are singing now with thanks and cheer.

About the Author

Danny Boy's body resides in England, but his heart and soul belong to Ireland. A loving husband and father with a passion for words in all forms. Outside of writing he finds solace and joy in his family and friends, movies, and thoughts of travel.

He is committed advocate and ambassador for mental health, working on a volunteer basis to support people with their battles, having battled his own traumas and demons his whole life.

Follow the author:
IG: @d.b.writes
FB: @dannyboywrites

Made in the USA
Las Vegas, NV
18 May 2022

49064875R00079